Royal Blunder and the Haunted House

That night a full moon shone through Julie's window. It woke her up and made her feel shivery. Darkness hid the garden like deep water. But there was someone golden sitting on the wall.

Julie crept downstairs and climbed on to the wall.

Royal Blunder's eyes shone in the moonlight, and his fur crackled with excitement.

"Have you come out to look for ghosts?" he asked.

HENRIETTA BRANFORD

Royal Blunder and the Haunted House

Illustrated by Lesley Harker

Scholastic Children's Books,
Commonwealth House, 1-19 New Oxford Street,
London WC1A 1NU, UK
a division of Scholastic Ltd
London ~ New York ~ Toronto ~ Sydney ~ Auckland
Mexico City ~ New Delhi ~ Hong Kong

Published in the UK by Scholastic Ltd, 1999

Text copyright © Henrietta Branford, 1994
Illustrations copyright © Lesley Harker, 1999

ISBN 0 590 65829 8

Typeset by Rowland Phototypesetting Ltd, Bury St Edmunds, Suffolk
Printed by Cox & Wyman Ltd, Reading, Berks.

2 4 6 8 10 9 7 5 3 1

Contents

Over the Wall
7

Fire! Fire!
13

Parrots Head Home
31

Julie and the Dentist
51

The Haunted House
65

Where Do Ghosts Go?
93

*For everyone who enjoyed
the first Royal Blunder book.*

Over the Wall

At the back of the street where Julie Jones lives, on the other side of everybody's walls and fences, lies a piece of waste ground. Long ago it was all woods round Julie's way but now it's streets and houses – all except the waste ground.

Sometimes an angry-looking person

with a ragged cloak and dirty fingernails passes that way. One or two wild creatures still live there, but most of them have left.

One summer evening as Julie was building a dam on the trickle of a stream that crossed the waste ground, two wild creatures crept out of a hole in the ground.

Their names were Mop and Mow. They were as pale as ghosties, with sharp eyes and claws like needles and horrid dangly feelers. When they saw Julie, they screeched at her.

"Wicked Bad!" screamed Mop. "You stole our Shiner!"

"Moon that shone for us below!" screeched Mow. "Taken from us long ago! Give it back to Mop and Mow!"

"Give it back, Wicked!"

Julie ran and Mop and Mow ran after her. "I didn't steal it!" she called over her shoulder. "It wasn't me!" She ran to the garden wall and pulled herself up on top of it.

"Wicked Bad!" screeched Mop from below. His sharp claws scraped against the wall. He stretched out a hairy arm and caught Julie by the foot. Julie kicked and tugged, but the harder she struggled, the tighter Mop held her foot.

"Royal Blunder!" Julie shouted. "Help! To me!"

The apple tree shook above Julie's head. Down from its branches Royal Blunder jumped, with his fur bristling and his eyes flashing and his pointed teeth glinting like daggers in the dark! And as he jumped, he grew – bigger and brighter and fiercer than any cat you've ever seen.

Mop and Mow took one look at him.

"Terrible teeth!" squeaked Mop, letting go of Julie's foot.

"Enormous big!" squeaked Mow.

They looked at one another. They

began to shake. Then they dropped off the wall and scuttled away into the night.

Royal Blunder sat down beside Julie. She leaned against him. His fur smelled of ginger; it felt warm and soft in the cool of the evening. Now that the danger was over, he looked like any other cat.

"That's that, Julie," he said. "They've gone."

And so they had.

Or had they?

Fire! Fire!

It was summer and the grass was dry and parched. Grasshoppers grated out their August music. Hidden in the long grass on the waste ground, Royal Blunder flexed his claws and turned his golden belly to the sun. After a while he rolled over to warm his back and lay with his paws dangling limply and his green eyes shut.

Meanwhile, in another part of the garden, Mr Lightfinger was working on his experiments. Mr Lightfinger was Julie's neighbour. He was doing his experiments in Julie's garden, in Julie's dad's shed, because his own shed was full of junk. His fiancée, Fuschia, had given him a super-de-luxe chemistry set for his birthday and he wanted to invent some really spectacular fireworks.

Julie had told her father that it was a bad idea to let Mr Lightfinger use the shed. She didn't trust him; but her father wouldn't listen.

Julie's parents had gone shopping. So had James and Jill and baby Jo. Julie didn't like shopping – she was supposed to stay next door and help Fuschia make a cake instead. But Fuschia got all bossy, so Julie decided to come home. In any case, she wanted to work on an experiment of her own, while everybody else was out.

She took Jill's magnifying glass. She took a stamp with a picture of a sailing ship on it from James's stamp album. She hadn't bothered to ask them if she could because she knew they'd say no.

She went out into the garden and put the stamp down on an old brick. She moved the magnifying glass carefully up and down until the sunlight fell in a bright drop on the mainsail. She held it steady until a tiny thread of smoke appeared. The sail wobbled in the heat. A black dot grew on it and the dot flickered into a flame.

"Fire!" whispered Julie. "All hands on deck!" The ship burned and the sea burned round it. Soon all that was left were some sooty black flakes which lifted off the brick and floated about in the warm summer air.

Julie stamped carefully on the sooty black flakes to make sure the fire was out. Then, leaving the magnifying glass lying on the ground, she climbed on to the wall.

"Where are you, Royal Blunder?" she called. "What are you doing?"

"I'm sleeping," said a voice from inside a clump of grass.

"It's very bright and hot today," called Julie. "Do you know why it's so bright and hot, Royal Blunder?"

"No."

"Because someone is looking at us through a magnifying glass. We could be burnt up into flakes of soot."

"Very likely," said Royal Blunder, without opening his eyes. His nose twitched. Two or three sparks blew up on a cloud of hot air behind Julie's back, but Royal Blunder did not see them.

Inside the shed a faint whiff of smoke tickled Mr Lightfinger's nose. He sneezed. He sneezed again. He came out of the shed, climbed over the garden fence, and went indoors to find a handkerchief. At the far end of the garden, the hens flew out of their run and perched in a row on the roof of Julie's house.

Down at the foot of the wall, small points of flame began to flicker all around the magnifying glass. They grew bigger and brighter surprisingly fast. Very soon they had licked and crackled right over to the shed. Inside the shed, things began to fizz and pop and bang. A fountain of hot sparks rose into the air, drifted a moment and hissed down on to Julie's head.

"Help!" shouted Julie. "Ouch! Something's burning me!"

Royal Blunder shot out of his clump of grass and with one flying leap, he landed on the wall, grabbed Julie by the scruff of her jumper and sprang with her over the flames and down into the garden.

"Quick!" he growled through a mouthful of jumper. "Call the fire brigade!"

Julie raced for the phone. Royal Blunder raced for the outside tap. He turned it on, picked up the hose in his powerful jaws and aimed the water at the burning shed. Jets of water began to squirt over the flames as Julie ran back to join him. "They're on their way!" she gasped. "The fire engine's coming!"

Sparks singed Royal Blunder's fur. Smoke stung Julie's eyes. The hens rose with a clatter from the roof and settled on the chimney pots. Not a moment too soon, Julie heard the wail of the siren and the screech of brakes as the big engine turned into her street.

It skidded to a halt just centimetres from the gate.

Uniformed fire-fighters jumped out and raced towards the fire, unfurling yellow fire hoses as they ran.

The Leading Fireman blew his whistle and the crew turned spouts of water on the burning shed. Naturally it took them a second or two to adjust their aim.

"Never mind your dress!" snapped Mr Lightfinger, as Fuschia wrung it out. "What about my experiments? What about my lovely fireworks?"

"Did someone mention fireworks?" asked the Leading Fireman.

There was an almighty roar followed by a clap of thunder and the first great rocket soared into the sky. A dozen others followed. Behind the apple tree the sky was filled with colours, scarlet and orange and gold and green. After the rockets came fountains and waterfalls and exploding balls of light. Curtains of swirling smoke opened and closed around the apple tree. Catherine wheels bounced across the vegetable patch, decimating the runner beans. The hens flew screeching from the chimney pots. As the shed began to split and crack apart, the whole front toppled outwards. It lurched towards Julie and Royal Blunder with a crackle and a roar. Before they could move, it had burst open in a shower of sparks.

The Leading Fireman just had time to pull Julie clear before the whole front of the shed fell on the very spot where she had been standing one second earlier. Alas, he had no time to do more. Royal Blunder disappeared behind a wall of smoke as a large part of the shed roof slid down on top of him.

Julie struggled to break free of the Leading Fireman's arms but he held her tightly. He did his best to comfort her but she would not be comforted. Soon her mother came flying down the garden path, followed by Jill and James and their father carrying baby Jo. They had heard the siren all the way from the Co-op, and seen the flames. Baby Jo was terribly excited.

"Julie! My darling! Are you really safe?" sobbed her mother, taking her from the Leading Fireman's arms. But Julie could not speak.

"There was a cat with her," the fire-fighter explained. "Brave as a lion he was. He stayed right beside your daughter and you know how cats hate fire. But I'm afraid he got caught when the roof fell in. I'm sorry. There was nothing we could do."

"Is there no chance he may have got away?" asked Julie's mother.

"There's always a chance with cats," said Julie's father, and the Leading Fireman nodded.

Julie's mother carried Julie into the house and put her to bed with a cup of camomile tea and a cold compress.

"We'll talk about how the fire started in the morning," she said. After that she sat on Julie's bed, not saying anything. Outside, the fire-fighters wound up their hoses.

Later that night, long after her mother had taken the cold compress off her forehead and put a hot-water bottle by her feet, Julie got out of bed. She wanted to be out of doors. She had thoughts to think that were too sad for bed. She crept downstairs and out into the old tin shelter. A smell of bonfires filled the night. Julie began to cry.

Presently, a smell of ginger and a whiff of spice floated in on the night air – a Royal Blunder smell. Was that the sound of paws padding towards her?

Could it be? Could it? Julie kept her eyes tight shut and sat perfectly still. A rough tongue began to lick the tears from her cheeks. A soft tail wound around her shoulders. Julie put her arms round Royal Blunder's neck and rubbed her nose against him.

"I'm sorry about my experiment," she said after a while. "It went wrong."

"They do sometimes," said Royal Blunder. "That's what they're for."

"My father will be cross about the shed," said Julie.

"Yes, I expect he will," said Royal Blunder. "But he'll be happy that you're safe."

Parrots Head Home

Julie sat on the garden wall thinking about parrots. Not pet-shop parrots, or parrots in zoos. No. Julie was thinking about wild parrots in far-off lands.

These were her favourite sorts: the Blue and Gold Macaw from the Amazon Basin; the Orange-Winged Amazon from Tobago; and the little

Eclectus parrot that lives on the island of Mindanao in the Sulu Sea.

From where she sat, Julie could see Royal Blunder prowling on the waste ground. He liked every kind of bird. Now and then he stopped to stalk one. When he got to the wall, he jumped up beside Julie. His tail hung down and rustled like a mouse in the ivy.

"I want to study parrots, Royal Blunder," Julie said.

A grasshopper landed on the wall. Royal Blunder caught it, chewed it, and swallowed the bits.

"I'd like to study parrots too," he said.

"What would you study, exactly?"

"Oh. This and that. One thing and another," said Royal Blunder, spitting out a sharp piece of grasshopper. "Be on the wall at sunset, Julie. And bring a sack."

Julie was there just before bedtime and so was Royal Blunder. Together they watched the stars come out. After that they jumped down on to the waste ground. Royal Blunder stood still while Julie climbed on to his back and he was off. He gathered in his power like a coiled spring. His stride grew longer and his big paws raised puffs of dust which hung behind him in the summer air as he leapt into the sky.

He flew until the island of Tobago lay below him like a speck in the ocean. Down there a joyful parrot squawked and swung in a palm tree. He had not a care in the world. Julie and Royal Blunder landed close beside him on the white sand of a Caribbean beach.

"Look, Royal Blunder," Julie whispered. "An Orange-Winged Amazon! What a beauty!"

Royal Blunder picked up the sack. He eased himself up the trunk of the palm tree as quietly as grass growing.

There was a squawk and a flurry, and the Orange-Winged Amazon parrot was in the sack.

"Royal Blunder!" Julie shouted. "What have you done?"

"Don't you want to stroke his feathers, Julie? Don't you want to feel his hooky beak?"

Julie did. His feathers felt like satin and his beak was as smooth as a nut.

"Let's keep him," Julie whispered. "We could catch a Blue and Gold Macaw next. And we could compare them properly before we let them go."

Soon they were down on the banks of the great River Amazon, where an ancient Macaw sang softly to herself a song of long ago.

Julie climbed skilfully up the tree. The Macaw took no notice of her. She was a deaf old bird, and she had never been particularly quick. One second she was sitting on a branch, and the next she was trapped in a sack with an angry young parrot from Tobago.

"We'll let you out soon," Julie told them. "We only want to look at you."

"One more?" suggested Royal Blunder. Julie nodded.

This time they flew until they reached the Sulu Sea. There below them lay a scatter of islands, gleaming softly in the evening light. Volcanic smoke trailed into the sky from the island of Mindanao. Wild forests covered the hills below. Down among the leafy fronds, two little Eclectus parrots had built a nest and hatched their chicks. The father had green feathers, the mother's were red. All that could be seen of the chicks were their little curved beaks, shining like polished toffee.

The hen bird screeched, the chicks fluttered and the little green cock bird bit and pecked; but he still ended up in the sack. "It's only for a little while," Julie whispered. "Then you'll be free again."

"Let's study them now," suggested Royal Blunder. "I can hardly wait to find out more about them." He sniffed at the sack and began to undo the string that fastened it.

"I wish we could take them home," said Julie. "Just for a day. There's a beautiful cage in our shed, a brass one. My grandad used to keep finches in it. The parrots would look lovely in that cage, Royal Blunder."

"OK," said Royal Blunder. "We'll take them home. I'll keep an eye on them tonight. You'll have all day tomorrow with them. In the evening we'll bring them back to where we found them."

"And let them go."

"Of course."

Back at the waste ground, Julie jumped off Royal Blunder's back and ran to fetch the big brass birdcage. She gave it a quick polish on her T-shirt and swept out the bits. Then she hung it from a branch of the willow tree beside the little stream.

Carefully, Julie let the parrots squeeze out of the sack and into the cage. Then she fastened the door and stood back. They looked magnificent. Bright and beautiful. Exotic and sad.

Julie went indoors. She was too excited to sleep; she lay in bed and thought about her wonderful parrots. At midnight she heard singing. She sat up and opened her window. Harsh foreign voices were singing, out on the waste ground.

"On leafy Tobago,
My dear island home,
In coconut places
Of tempest and foam,
My sweet nest lies waiting.
Oh, let me go home!"

Everything was quiet for a minute; then a quavering voice floated over the wall.

"Remember the river
Where rain forests blow,
Dark river Amazon,
There let me go!
Old is the river,
Old, old am I.
Dark river Amazon,
There let me die."

The third song was the saddest of all.

"On far Mindanao,
In the blue Sulu Sea,
My love and my hatchlings
Are calling for me.
My red-feathered hen
And my hatchlings three
Wait on far Mindanao,
In the warm Sulu Sea."

Julie got out of bed and went quietly downstairs. She crossed the garden and climbed over the wall. Out on the waste ground, under the willow tree, she found Royal Blunder and the parrots.

"I didn't know how sad they'd be," she said to Royal Blunder.

He didn't answer. He was looking at the parrots.

"I must let them go home at once," said Julie.

Still Royal Blunder didn't answer.

"*Now*, Royal Blunder."

"I don't think. . ." Royal Blunder began.

But Julie had already opened the door of the cage.

Out came the parrots, fluttering and hopping in the chilly English night. They perched in the branches of the willow tree and shook out their shining feathers. The Eclectus parrot was last to emerge. He cocked a round eye at the stars. He seemed to be thinking. Julie wanted to stroke his feathers one last time, but he was too quick for her. With an angry clatter of wings he shot out of the tree. The other two followed, fast as arrows, and away they went – the Eclectus parrot in the lead, with the Orange-Winged Amazon next, and the old lady Macaw last. One green feather floated softly down and landed at Julie's feet.

"I don't think you should have done that, Julie," said Royal Blunder.

Two days later, at breakfast time, Julie and her dad were looking at the papers.

"You're keen on rare birds, aren't you, Julie?" said her dad. Julie nodded. "Listen to this then: 'BEAUTIFUL BIRDS FLY SOUTH. FEATHERED FUGITIVES SPOTTED AT SEA.'

It says that members of the Royal Society for Spotting Rare Birds have been monitoring three rare parrots — they reckon they've escaped from somewhere."

"Do you think they'll get home, Dad?"

"No. Even if they knew the way, they couldn't fly that far."

That night, Julie cried in her bed. If only we'd left them alone, she thought, they'd be safe now if we had. Safe and happy, doing the things that parrots do. She opened her window and looked out, but the garden was empty.

Next day she took the paper out into the garden. FEATHERED FUGITIVES IN FLIGHT TO FREEDOM! she read. PARROTS HEAD HOME! BIRD SPOTTERS TRACK BLUE AND GOLD MACAW TO AMAZON BASIN, she read. ORANGE-WINGED AMAZON PARROT TOUCHES DOWN ON TOBAGO, she read. SEA CAPTAIN REPORTS TYPHOON OVER SOUTH CHINA SEA, she read.

ECLECTUS PARROT FEARED LOST AT SEA.

Julie put down the paper and climbed into the apple tree. She thought about the Eclectus parrot. She thought about his green feathers and his round dark eyes. She thought about the red hen bird and the chicks with their beaks like polished toffee and she began to cry all over again. Her nose was getting sore.

Presently Royal Blunder climbed into the apple tree. He rubbed his ear against her salty cheek.

"Why are you crying, Julie?" he asked.

"He didn't make it. The Eclectus parrot. There was a typhoon. In the South China Sea. He must be dead by now."

"He's not."

"How do you know, Royal Blunder?"

"I heard him singing, Julie. Late last night, from all across the world. He's home."

Julie and the Dentist

"I don't want to go to the dentist, Mum."

"I know. But you've got to, Julie. It'll be all right."

"It won't."

Julie went into the garden and sat by herself in the hollow place in the hedge. She could hear James and Jill getting their kites out of the shed.

They were going to the park. Baby Jo was going too.

Presently Royal Blunder came stepping along the top of the garden wall, as bright as a banner in the sun. Julie closed her eyes and wished. A few seconds later there was a rustle in the hedge.

"Hello, Royal Blunder," said Julie. "Have you come to tell me I don't have to go to the dentist?"

"No," said Royal Blunder, "I haven't."

"Sometimes, Royal Blunder, you seem like just an ordinary cat to me."

Royal Blunder did not reply. He sat in a patch of sunshine washing his golden fur, as cats do when they are annoyed.

"Julie! It's time to go!" called her mother.

Julie stood up. Royal Blunder stood up too. Gently he touched his nose to hers. "Good luck with the dentist," he said.

The smell of medicine wafted out the moment Julie opened the door of the Health Centre, making her feel sick.

She went over to the waiting area and sat down. Soon the nurse came over. She smiled at Julie. She looked all right.

"There's a new dentist here today," she said. "I haven't met her yet, but I'm sure you'll like her. You can go along to her room now."

Julie held herself straight and stiff and tried to ignore the bees buzzing in her belly. The door at the end of the corridor was open. She peeped in. What she saw inside that room was ghastly.

Ahead of her loomed the dentist's chair. On one side of it stood a shiny metal basin which made horrible sucking and swallowing noises. Beside that was a thing like a robot with stabbers and grabbers and long metal arms. Beside the robot stood someone even worse. Her teeth were unbelievable – Julie could see great black cavities in them from right across the room! Instead of a clean white dentist's overall, this person wore a ragged cloak. Her fingernails were rimmed with dirt and in her hand she held a bag of peppermints.

"Come here, little girl," she croaked. She kicked the door shut, leaving Julie's mother on the other side of it. "Sit down in my nice chair and have some sweets. A little bit of sugar does your teeth no end of good."

Now Julie may have been young, but she was nobody's fool. She knew at once this *could not* be the dentist. She knew a witch when she saw one.

"Come here," whispered the witch.

"No!" shouted Julie. "Never!"

The room grew very quiet. Outside the window, trees waved in the wind. Buses went past on the road and Julie could see her mother's car parked in the car park, but it all seemed very far away.

"I don't think you know any magic," whispered the witch.

But she was wrong. Julie took a deep breath, filling her powerful lungs. "Royal Blunder!" she shouted. "Royal Blunder! To me!"

The witch took no notice. Stretching out a long arm, she pointed an evil-looking wand at Julie. Quick as a flash, Julie leapt across the room. She grabbed the tube with the funnel on the end from the sucking and swallowing basin, pressed a button on the side, and pointed the contraption straight at the witch's wand. There was a loud gobbling sound and the wand shot out of the witch's hand and hurtled across the room, smack into the funnel. Down the tube it plunged and into the plug-hole. There was an extra-loud sucking and swallowing noise, followed by a belch. The witch leapt across the room with a scream of rage. She grabbed Julie by the shoulders and began to shake her cruelly.

Before she could do any more, a crash and a smash shook the Health Centre. Fragments of bright, shiny glass cascaded in every direction as Royal Blunder hurtled through the window! His ears lay flat against his mighty head and his lips were drawn back from his teeth. "Get away from Julie this instant, Bonebeneath!" he snarled. He bounded across the room, scattering sets of false teeth and trays of instruments in every direction.

Bonebeneath gasped. Fear paralysed her for a second. Then she snapped her fingers and murmured a spell. Her broomstick shot out of a locker, flew across the room and landed smack in her hand. After that, she moved so fast that all Julie could see was a black streak skimming across the room and out through the broken window.

When she reached the height of five hundred metres, Bonebeneath began to empty her pockets. "Bombs away!" she cried, and down rained a selection of the most revolting stuff. Used paper hankies. Damp chewing-gum. Half a Chinese takeaway. Egg sandwiches, ear wax, hairy spiders, and worse. People who chanced to look up were astonished to see her streak across the sky. They were even more astonished when horrible things began to drift down over pavements and playgrounds city-wide. Cries of "Eugh!" "Yuk!" and "Oh, pooh!" rang through the town.

Back at the Health Centre, Julie and Royal Blunder were clearing up the mess.

"You know who that was, don't you?" said Royal Blunder.

Julie nodded. "What was she doing here?" she said.

"Just being horrible. It's her way of having fun."

"Will she come back?"

"She might."

Royal Blunder winked at the shattered window. There was a quiet chinking sound and the shining fragments of glass whirled into place, leaving the window perfectly repaired.

"Hadn't you better let your mother in now?" he asked.

Julie opened the surgery door and

her mother rushed into the room.

"Julie, darling!" she gasped. "Are you all right? I heard such strange noises! And the door seemed to be locked!" She kissed Julie and hugged her tightly. Behind her waited a woman in a clean white coat.

"How do you do, Julie?" she said. "I'm your new dentist. I'd like to look at your teeth, please."

Julie climbed into the dentist's chair. She laid her head on the headrest, opened her mouth, and looked out of the window at the autumn trees. High in the tallest one she could just see a splash of yellow gold.

The Haunted House

Julie didn't like going past the empty house at the end of her street, especially not at night, when there were thick black shadows between the parked cars on the road. She felt as if there was somebody inside that house – somebody inside, looking out.

"I wish someone would buy that

house," she told her brother.

"Nobody will," said James. "Someone was murdered there. It's haunted. If you spend the night there you can hear the victim shrieking."

"You've never even been inside."

"I'm going to, though. Alone. I'm going to stay all night."

"Ignore him, Julie," said their mother. "He's just trying to frighten you. And James, you know you mustn't go inside."

"Why not?"

"There could be a tramp there. Or the floor might be rotten. Or the roof might fall in on your head."

"Anyway," said Julie, "it's not our house."

"Quite right, Julie," her mother agreed.

"Whose house is it?" James asked.

"It used to belong to a funny old woman with long white plaits. But that was years ago."

Julie couldn't stop thinking about the empty house. She asked the postman, the milkman and the dustbin lady why it was empty.

"A mad woman used to live there," said the postman. "She had a black dog that would have took my arm off if she'd ever had a letter. Which she didn't."

"So you never actually saw her, then?" asked Julie.

"No," sighed the postman. "I never."

"A hunch-backed man with a hook on the end of his arm used to live there," said the milkman. "I'd have been scared to death if he'd ordered owt off my float. Which he never."

"So you didn't actually meet him?" asked Julie. The milkman shook his head.

"Somebody with a bin full of bones lived in that house," muttered the dustbin lady. "We used to hear 'em rattling. But we never stopped to pick 'em up."

"So you never saw the bones then?"

"Saw 'em, no," said the dustbin lady. "Heard 'em, yes."

Julie told Royal Blunder what the postman, the milkman and the dustbin lady had told her. "But I don't believe them," she added. "They're making up stories, just like my brother."

"Interesting stories, aren't they?" said Royal Blunder. "Don't they make you want to take a look in that house?"

"No," said Julie. "They don't."

"Full moon would be best, if it is haunted. Ghosts flock to a full moon."

That night a full moon shone through Julie's window. It woke her up and made her feel shivery. Darkness hid the garden like deep water. But there was someone golden sitting on the wall.

Julie crept downstairs. She took a clove of garlic from the kitchen window-sill to protect her from vampires. She took a twig from the spindleberry tree by the door to keep witches away. Then she climbed on to the wall.

Royal Blunder's eyes shone in the moonlight, and his fur crackled with excitement.

"Have you come out to look for ghosts?" he asked.

Julie shook her head.

"Are you frightened of ghosts, Julie?"

"Yes."

"I don't know why you should be — most of them are only shadows. Some are messengers. Some come back to visit favourite places. Some of them come because they need our help, and some because they want to help us. Mostly we pass each other by and hardly notice one another. Even a spiteful ghost can't do much harm. But if you're frightened, we won't go."

"Have you actually *seen* a ghost, Royal Blunder?"

"I see them all the time. Because of being out at night."

Royal Blunder stood up and stretched himself in the moonlight. He seemed to grow larger as Julie watched. When he jumped down into the flowerbed, Julie could only just reach to climb on to his back. She gripped his furry flanks with her knees to stop herself slipping as he carried her through the dark garden and out into the night. At the dark end of the street, the empty house waited.

Royal Blunder slipped past the broken gate and down into the garden. Tall rose bushes tangled over a tumbledown fence. The grass on the lawn came up to Royal Blunder's shoulders and tickled Julie's knees. A box tree that had once been neatly clipped into a lollipop had sprouted tentacles and turned into an octopus. The whole place felt well and truly haunted.

A broken bench leaned by the back door, beside a garden table all patterned with moss. A bunch of flowers stood on the table in a little china jug. Beside the flowers lay a pair of rusty secateurs. Under the bench were two small boots.

Julie slid off Royal Blunder's back.

She looked curiously at the flowers, the secateurs and the boots. She tiptoed over to the kitchen window and peeped in. A tattered coat hung over the back of a chair. She remembered what her mother had said about tramps. But would a tramp pick flowers? Or have such very small feet?

Before she could ask Royal Blunder what he thought, they both heard a thud and a thump from inside the house. Quietly, Royal Blunder pushed the back door open and went in.

Julie's legs felt heavy and cold. Her chest felt tight but she did not want to stay in the haunted garden on her own, so she followed him in. Both of them heard a tiny sound, coming from upstairs … the sound of someone breathing in the dark.

Royal Blunder slid silently upstairs. Julie tiptoed after him holding tightly to his tail. The first door they came to was open. Peeping in, Julie saw an ancient, dusty bedroom. There was a four-poster bed with a wobbly arrangement of boxes beside it. The boxes had tipped over and lay scattered on the floor. There was a fireplace with a faded hearth-rug. On the hearth-rug lay something that looked like a bundle of sooty rags.

The rags moved. A hand crept out from them. Julie saw that the bundle was a little old woman, all covered in soot and scratches. She looked as if she'd fallen down the chimney.

"Who are you?" asked the old woman. "What are you doing in my house?"

"We didn't know it was your house. We thought it was empty," Julie stammered.

The old woman got slowly to her feet and brushed off some of the soot. "You mean you thought it was haunted," she said.

Julie nodded. "Shall we help you get back into bed, now we're here?" she asked.

"You may as well. I can't seem to manage my boxes."

The old woman was as light as feathers. Lighter. Her voice was nothing but a whisper of dead leaves. Her hands were like ice. But her grey eyes were shining.

"What were you trying to do?" Julie asked. "When you fell over? Only we might be able to help you."

The old lady shook her head. "I doubt it," she said sadly. "But get under my eiderdown and I'll tell you how I came to fall over."

Julie and Royal Blunder made themselves comfortable at the foot of the four-poster bed while the old woman arranged her pillows. Julie could see her wrinkled face and her long white plaits by the light of the moon.

"Long ago," she began, "back-along, down-along, faraway-off, when I was a child and my plaits just reached my shoulders, I went a-walking in the woods, one night of the full moon. Alone I went, although my mother said I never should. I went to see the rabbits hop and nibble. But it wasn't rabbits that I saw."

"What was it?" whispered Julie. "Was it ghosts?"

"That I don't know for sure. It was two little creatures. Pale, they were, with claws that pattered on the ground, and snaily feelers on their heads. They made my skin crawl. Came out of a hole in the ground, they did, talking to one another in sharp little voices so high I couldn't hardly hear 'em. They were nudging and shoving one another, running this way and that. Agitated, they were, and carrying something between 'em. Something that shone like a lantern."

Julie wanted to say something, but the old woman went on with her story.

"All of a sudden, I sneezed. Couldn't help myself. And those creatures dropped their lantern and scuttled back down their hole. That's how I came to steal it. But it wasn't a lantern. It was jewels. It was moonstone and sapphire, water and ice, shining in the palm of my hand. Well. Pretty soon those creatures came back up, twittering something about the moon, and *give it back*. Desperate, they seemed."

"And you didn't give their jewels back?" asked Julie.

The old woman shook her head. "I held 'em up high, and I looked at 'em, and the more I looked, the more I wanted to keep 'em. I told myself I'd only keep 'em for a day or two. And off I ran. The creatures came after me but I could run like the wind when I was little. Night after night I heard 'em weeping and cheeping under my windows as though their wild, wicked hearts would break, begging and beseeching me to give back their treasure. But I wouldn't."

There was a silence, and then a sniff. Tears glittered on the old woman's cheeks. "Pretty soon I began to be sorry. I knew it was wrong. I'd have put it right, if I could have. But they stopped calling under my window and I never heard their voices any more. I have grown old waiting to give back what I took from those unhappy creatures."

"Where did you put their treasure?" Julie asked.

"Up the chimney. I wanted to fetch it down one last time, but I can't reach it any more."

Royal Blunder got out of the warm nest he'd made under the eiderdown. He looked at the old woman, and she nodded. A few minutes later he was washing the smuts from his fur and the treasure was lying between them on the eiderdown like a puddle of light.

It was a moonstone the size of an egg, and in the centre of it, sparkling and shimmering like light under water was a sapphire.

"I can see why they wanted it back," Julie said.

"But it's too late," sighed the old woman. "It all happened so long ago. Those wild creatures must be dead and gone by now."

"They're not! They're still alive. And I know where they are!" said Julie. "They live on the waste ground behind the street! I know they do because I saw them there. They saw me too. They called me wicked. They chased me and I was scared. But we can take the treasure back to them, if you want us to."

The old woman lay back on her pillows and closed her eyes. A smile spread all around her face and she seemed to Julie to grow younger – not less wrinkly, but happier and wider awake. "Would you?" she whispered. "Could you?"

Five minutes later, Julie and Royal Blunder were springing through the haunted garden, over the tumbledown fence and out on to the waste ground. Royal Blunder headed for the part where a dark mouth opened in the ground and a tunnel ran deep underground.

Deep down under, they stopped still, listening. Julie took the treasure out of her pocket and held it up. A grey-blue light shone out of it and lit the cave. Sharp claws came pattering. Small voices scolded, sharp as needles in the dark.

"Quick, Mow! Hurry! Mop can feel the blue moon shining!"

"Reckless, feckless Mop! Mop feels the moon! Mow feels the cat!"

Mow hung back, muttering, but Mop raced past him, wild with excitement, stumbling out of the tunnel and into the light that streamed from Julie's hand.

"Moon belong to Mop and Mow!" he squeaked. "Taken from us long ago! Give it back to Mop and Mow!"

Julie leaned down from Royal
Blunder's back and held her hand out
towards Mop, keeping a sharp eye on
his pointed claws.

"Wicked thief!" Mop scolded.
"Wicked Bad!"

"It wasn't me," Julie told him. "And
the thief is sorry. She's been sorry for a
long time. She's an old woman now."

Mop grunted. He took the moonstone, cupped it in his hairy hands and stared into the sapphire. Then he turned and put the treasure into Mow's hand. He looked up and Julie caught a glimpse of triumph on his face. "Mop and Mow's tunnel," he spat. "Go away, Wicked. Get out. Cat go, too. Mop and Mow stay safe below."

"You know that empty house, Julie?" her mother said, a few days later. "The one you don't like going past?"

"I used not to like it. I don't mind it now."

"No? Well, I saw some children in the garden, and I met their mother in the post office today. She's bought the house. It won't be empty any more."

"It isn't empty now, Mum. The old woman lives there. The old woman with long white plaits. I met her."

"You can't have, Julie. It's not possible."

"I did, Mum."

Julie's mother shook her head. "There used to be an old woman with plaits, Julie. She lived there years ago. I told you, she owned the house. Remember? But you can't have met her, Julie. She died before you were born."

Where Do Ghosts Go?

Julie's mother had a puzzled look on her face as she came downstairs after saying good night. Upstairs in her bed, Julie was puzzled too. She opened her window and looked out. The moon was gone, and the waste ground was invisible. But there was still a dash of gold on the wall.

"Royal Blunder," she called. The dash of gold sat up and Julie saw a flash of green as Royal Blunder blinked at her. "Royal Blunder, where has the old woman gone?"

"She's gone where ghosts go when the moon wanes, Julie."

"Will I see her again?"

"I don't think so."

Royal Blunder stood up and paced along the garden wall.

"Where are you going?" Julie called.

"Hunting."

"But will she be happy, Royal Blunder? Will she be happy and well?"

"Yes, Julie. She will be well. The moon will return, and she will be well."

Royal Blunder began to run along the top of the wall. With each stride he went a little faster until, when he got

to the corner, he was running, leaping, loping like a tongue of flame along the wall. Right at the corner, he jumped.

Julie watched him, bright and burning in the darkness, until all that remained was the pattern of sparks left by his paws in the sky.

The End